Where Are You?

A Child's book about Loss

By Laura Olivieri
Illustrated by Kristin Elder

In heartfelt memory of Jose; may you find love and love find you, wherever you are…

For my beautiful son Chayton; I love you more than a power ranger, strawberry-peach pie, and the whole universe.

And for my Gram and the Serenity Prayer she cherishes and has taught me.   You are right here.

It is our ongoing wish that this book bring comfort and kindness to all who read it

Where are you, now that you are gone?

We took your body to a special place, to say goodbye.

But you were not there. I was Sad.

I look at your picture and your blue shirt in the closet.

But you are not here. I miss you.

Maybe you are an angel now with beautiful wings.

But I cannot see you.

Maybe you are in a happy place like warm sunshine
that makes you giggle.

But I cannot hear you.

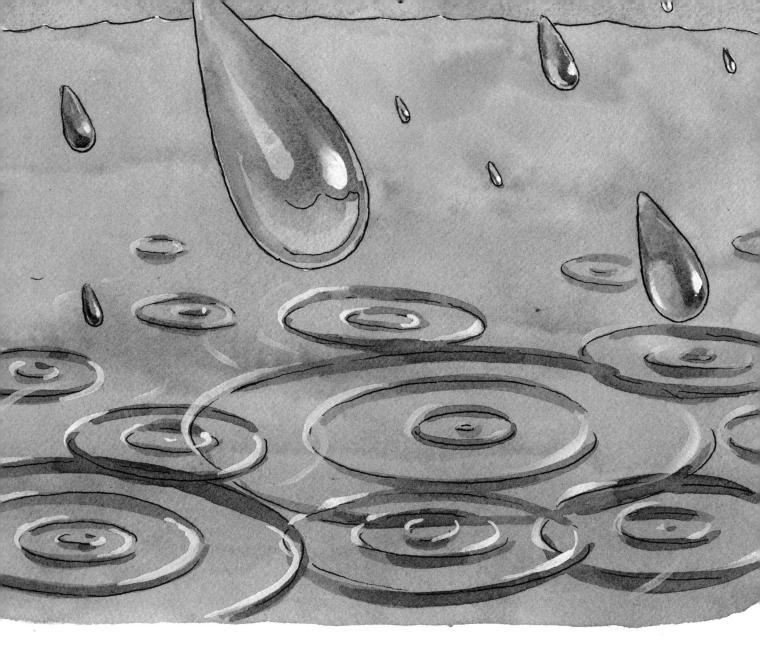

Maybe you are a raindrop that fell into the cool blue ocean.

But I cannot touch you.

I drew a picture of us when we were together.
I smiled when I made it.

I think of all the stuff we did, when we played and laughed so hard. I was happy.

And when you made me sit at the table and finish my vegetables, even when I didn't want to…

because you love me.

I remember you.

So you are right here.

Special Thanks to
Our Wonderful Sponsors

Steven, Ashley and Kennedy Ochs

Jose Olivieri and Beverly Geyer

Patricia and Gilbert Line

Beverly Flowers-Coleman

Jon and April Nold

I would like to thank all of our family, friends and coworkers who supported us through this difficult time, our ongoing recovery and the completion of this project. Your kindness, friendship and love have meant the world to us, are cherished, and will not be forgotten.

About the Subject
Talking to young children about death

My son was three when his father died. I was overwhelmed at the thought of telling him and explaining things. I tried to find a children's book on the subject to help me, but most books were designed for older children.

Young children do not have the ability to understand abstract ideas, things that are intangible, in the same way adults do. What I found is that my son asks me questions as he is able to process ideas. As he matures, the questions change. In that process I am learning I must first answer these questions for myself, before I can answer him.

My best advice on dealing with this most sensitive and universal subject is to be kind, truthful and available. Explain things simply, without graphic detail. Most children will indicate what they need to know, when they need to know it and when they have had enough.

Your guidance during this time is the most crucial guidance your child may ever need. Beyond your support, you may also find counseling or therapy with a trained professional necessary.

What you believe about what happens after death may differ from the ideas in this book. I have tried to allow room for everyone in this text. Share your own beliefs with your children as you will.

About the Author
Laura Olivieri

I am a mom. I am not a child psychologist, therapist or doctor. I have no degree and hold no qualification to advise parents on raising children. What I do have to offer is my own experience.

In 2003, after many deteriorating years of marriage, I decided to divorce my husband. During that process he committed suicide, leaving me with my wonderful three-year-old son, who would now never know his father.

I have learned many things from this experience; compassion, kindness, self-reliance and responsibility among them.

Despite these circumstances, raising a child in a supportive environment, so that he can grow up to be a healthy, responsible and happy person, is my primary goal and ongoing challenge.

CPSIA information can be obtained
at www.ICGtesting.com
Printed in the USA
LVIC06n0522310517
536403LV00024B/485